THE USED-TO-BE BEST FRIEND

DAWN QUIGLEY

THE USED-TO-BE BEST FRIEND

ILLUSTRATED BY
TARA AUDIBERT

Heartdrum
An Imprint of HarperCollinsPublishers

Heartdrum is an imprint of HarperCollins Publishers.

Jo Jo Makoons: The Used-to-Be Best Friend
Text copyright © 2021 by Dawn Quigley
Illustrations copyright © 2021 by Tara Audibert
All rights reserved. Printed in the United States of America.
No part of this book may be used or reproduced in any manner
whatsoever without written permission except in the case of brief
quotations embodied in critical articles and reviews. For infor-
mation address HarperCollins Children's Books, a division of
HarperCollins Publishers, 195 Broadway, New York, NY 10007.
www.harpercollinschildrens.com

Library of Congress Control Number: 2020952904
ISBN 978-0-06-301537-1 (trade bdg.)
ISBN 978-0-06-301538-8 (pbk.)

Typography by Andrea Vandergrift
21 22 23 24 25   PC/LSCC   10 9 8 7 6 5 4 3 2 1
❖
First Edition

ABOUT THIS STORY

Jo Jo lives on a fictional Native American Ojibwe reservation, the Pembina Ojibwe Reservation. A reservation is land under the care of a Native Nation that calls it home. The land now called the United States is home to more than three hundred reservations and over five hundred Tribal Nations. There are many reservations in the United States, but Jo Jo's is not an actual one. Every reservation has unique and special elements, and Jo Jo's reservation incorporates many of those found in Ojibwe (and many other Native American) communities.

KOKUM

MIMI

MOM

JOJO

FERN

CHUCK

SUSAN

TEACHER

BRIE

FERRIS

JIM

CONTENTS

Best Friend #1

"**G**oodbye, Mimi," I said as I walked past her on the way toward the front door.

Mimi:

"I said *goodbye*, Mimi! I'll miss you!" I even threw some air kisses to her.

Mimi only turned her head away from me.

"Mimi, you will always be my best friend number one!"

Mimi:

Why is it she won't ever reply? Or let me

know she'll miss *me* when I'm gone? I know I'll miss her.

We do this every day. 'Cause I have to leave every day. Well, most days. Mama says it's the law.

There should be a law about not saying goodbye to your first *best friend*. The one who has to go to school *every* day. Every day!

I think I would like more friends. At least ones who will answer me.

But cats are *very* good home friends. They are already potty-trained. They are very clean. And they even will take you on a walk.

I have a home best friend, and I used to have a school best friend.

But I don't think my school best friend wants to be *my* best friend anymore. I think I need more pals. Just in case.

Let me tell you about myself. I am seven years old and in the first grade. My name is Jo Jo Makoons Azure. You wanna know another way of saying that, in Ojibwe? (That's the name of my Native American tribe!) Try saying: "Jo Jo Makoons Azure nindizhinikaaz."

Big last word, right? You sound out that last word like this: nin-DEZH-in-i-kauz.

Got it? If you can say *Tyrannosaurus rex*, you can say *nindizhinikaaz*.

But my real big name is Josephine Makoons Azure. Mama says Moushoom gave me the name Makoons because when I was a baby, I growled and had short black hair—just like a little bear cub! You say *Makoons* like this: ma-KOONS.

Do you wanna know what *moushoom* means? It means "grandpa" in the Michif language. Michif is one kind of Native American language. But it is a language made from words that are Cree, French, and Ojibwe. We speak many languages on our reservation.

Ojibwe is my Native American tribe. You say it like this: oh-JIB-way. See? Ojibwe.

I'm learning my Ojibwe language because I'm a member of the Pembina Ojibwe Nation. I like to learn to speak Ojibwe and Michif.

I asked Mama, "What's the difference between Ojibwe and Michif?"

"Well, my girl, think of Michif like a part of the big, beautiful Ojibwe world."

* * *

Mama says I have strong lungs. But Grandpa also said I will grow up to be strong, like a bear. Except I only hear my full, big, fancy name from Mama when I'm in trouble.

"Josephine Makoons Azure, why is grape juice all over my beading?"

"Josephine Makoons Azure, why are the toes cut out of *all* the new socks I bought you?"

Mama likes to ask me these silly questions. But I think the answers should be kind of easy to figure out. Like Tuesday, I was drinking grape juice (outside the kitchen, which I'm not supposed to do). I was looking at the beaded leather jewelry Mama was working on for the summer powwow trail.

When I tried to get a closer look at it, I spilled my drink all over the table.

Mama's always telling me *not* to get the fancy living room carpet dirty. So, before the grape juice could run off the table, I mopped it up with the closest thing: her leather jewelry.

And she never even thanked me for saving the carpet from grape juice, which is a *very* hard stain to get out!

And her sock question? I like to sleep with socks on every night. Even in the summer. But my toes get hot because Mimi's always sleeping on my feet. Which is why I have my "night socks." They have the toes cut out (after the socks get stinky and stretched out). Mama always says to save things instead of throwing them away. So I glued together all the sock toes and used it for her Mother's Day present. It's a pot-holder quilt! But, shh, don't tell her. It's a surprise!

Back to Mimi (my home best friend who ignores me sometimes). I have to catch the school bus every morning. Mama usually walks with me, but today my kokum was going to. *Kokum* is another way to say "grandma" in the Michif language. She moved in with us after my moushoom died last year. She said at her old place the quiet was too loud without Moushoom.

Sometimes I worry about my kokum's way of thinking. How can a place be too loud with one less person in it? But I miss my moushoom. We told stories together. He liked my stories best—of any he'd ever heard.

This school morning, by the front door, Mama and Grandma had a funny conversation. They were whispering. But I heard because I was hiding in the coat closet. Not really secret hiding, but like a spy. I like to hang out in there sometimes. I dug through Grandma's coat

pockets to search for her hard candy.

She likes to eat candy. But Mama tells her it's bad for her die-beeties. I do not know what that is, but Kokum smells like cherry Life Savers. It is a very pretty smell.

That's when I heard them.

"Who's taking her? I can't see anymore to drive through town," Grandma said.

Mama answered, "No, Ma, I will. Spring's here and she needs them. We can't let her outside without them."

Grandma replied, "Oh, we'll have to trick her into going. You know she hates shots."

I think maybe spying isn't all that great. Because I just heard them saying that Mimi needed shots. I used to not like that word. But last summer, when I needed shots, Kokum told me, "My girl, shots help you to be very healthy. There are many sicknesses out there, and shots give good protection. We want Mimi to get shots because we love her and want her to be healthy, just like we make sure you get shots because we love you and want you to be healthy."

Ferris, my bus friend, said last week that if a cat gets a shot, sometimes it lets all the air out of their body. Just like a balloon letting the air out.

"Jo Jo, all that's left of a cat is a pile of skin. All because of a shot," Ferris told me.

I do not know if I believe Ferris. But he is very smart about balloons. It was very nice of him to tell me this.

I sneaked out of the closet after Mama left. I grabbed my backpack. And grabbed my best friend #1. If Mimi had to get shots, she wasn't doing it alone. Or at all.

Best Friend #2

My other best friend is Fern. Fern is my school best friend. Do you know what a school best friend is? It's a best friend at school who will play with you at recess. Also, a school best friend will sit with you at lunch and give you half her sandwich when your mom packs a tuna-fish sandwich.

I do not like tuna fish. Sometimes I think Mama gets my lunch and Mimi's lunch mixed up.

Fern was waiting for me when I got off the

bus. We're both in the first grade at Little Shell Elementary School. We live on the Pembina Reservation. I've lived here my whole life. Fern just moved here last year with her auntie.

We've been school best friends ever since. But lately, Fern hasn't been sitting with me at lunch every day. And it makes me sad because Fern makes me happy. When I sit by myself, I crouch my back over so my head is right in my lunch bag. Then no one can see me.

"Jo Jo, hi! It's hot, enit?" Fern said.

"I like it!" I answered.

Fern kind of likes talking about the weather. A lot. Kokum says that's what people from the Midwest talk about. Not sure about that. But, when it rains it pours, I guess. My kokum says that all the time.

We walked down to our classroom. Teacher was waiting by the door for us. Oops, I forgot, I'm not supposed to call him Teacher. He says everyone's name is important. And that we should use people's specific names.

But he *is* my teacher. That's why I call him Teacher.

"Boozhoo, Fern and Josephine." Teacher nodded as we walked in. That's how Teacher says hello to us in Ojibwe.

"Boozhoo, Mr. Welch," Fern and I answered. That's how Fern and me say hello to Teacher.

Boozhoo means "hello" in Ojibwe. Can you say it, too? It's like this: BOO-zhoo.

Teacher tries to use our Ojibwe words every morning. It sounds more like he's choking on a bunch of marbles. His words don't sound like the way the elders say them. Teacher isn't Native American. He didn't grow up hearing or speaking our language. But he's trying. I would give him a C+ for trying. And maybe a smiley face.

Teacher isn't like us. Mama says I shouldn't say that. But his skin is pink. He calls it "white."

On my reservation, my Ojibwe people are all shades—light, dark, and brown. Our hair can be blond, black, brown, or red. But most of us are brown.

My skin is brown. "Lovely brown. Beautiful brown," Mama calls us. I like that. Because we are beautiful. Brown like the soil Moushoom used to plant our sweet corn in. Brown like the leather Mama uses to bead barrettes on. Brown like the fry bread for our family feasts.

Brown is my favorite color. After polka dots.

At school, we have reading right away in the morning. I'm better at math. I can see numbers and how they work together. Like, I get how 2 + 2 = 4. See, if my mama gives me two pieces of fry bread, then Kokum makes two more, we all have four to share. But Teacher's math seems like it's only for one person. I like to do math thinking about my Ojibwe community. Like last week Teacher asked us to think about a math problem: *Five people want to eat a bunch of four bananas. Each person can have only one. How many people don't get a banana?*

I answered, "Everyone gets some banana."

Teacher shook his head no. He said that *one* person would not get any banana.

"But we all *share* what we have," I said. "That's what Native people do."

Teacher didn't say anything after that. See? I'm good at math.

But reading and writing? That does not make too much sense to me. Teacher calls reading time "language arts" time. But that is a funny name because I like learning about my Native American language. We're Ojibwe, remember?

One day when Teacher said it was time for language arts, I said to him, "Boozhoo." And then I drew a picture of me saying "hello" to Teacher. You know, because it's "language + arts" time.

But Teacher shook his head. "Okay, Jo Jo, let's try this again. No Ojibwe, no art. It's *language arts* time."

"But, Teacher, I love *our* language and

our art." Not sure why he tilted his head and looked at me with real big eyes. Then he took out a tissue to wipe his eyes after I said that. Must be what Kokum calls allergic. Kokum says she's allergic to tree pollen. Tree pollen bothers her nose and she feels icky around it. So, during *Teacher's* "language arts" time (where there was *no* art and *no* Ojibwe), he wanted us to work on rhymes. Teacher says rhymes can help us to read and write.

"Children," Teacher said, "I would like all of you to go to the table and write your very own rhymes. Be sure to show them to me."

Rhyme Time

Fern and I sat at the same table. Teacher calls it the Blue Table. I call it the "Kids Kicked Out of the Red Table 'Cause We Can't Read So Good" table. But I like it here. Fern is here. But so is Chuck. I call him Up-Chuck. Teacher does not like that. I guess Up-Chuck shouldn't have thrown up on the first day of school, then. Teacher says I shouldn't call him that.

But Up-Chuck always does a big belly laugh when I say it. Sometimes he even writes

19

that on his worksheets as his name. But he also adds a little drawing of himself chucking up. He is a very good artist.

We sat down to write our own rhymes.

Fern wrote: *The dish would wish for a fish.*

I looked at her, and right away she said, "See, Jo Jo, it's easy. You try."

Chuck wrote: *Dog jogged on the log.*

Okay, his was not very good. But Teacher liked it enough that he got a sticker! AND it was a shiny one.

Do you know about star stickers? Other than glittery pencils, stickers are the most special thing a teacher can ever give you. Well, you might think a plus sign or smiley face is great, too. But a teacher has to actually *lick* a star sticker. I mean, they use their own *spit*. So it's kind of a big deal. It must mean you're a good student.

If there were stickers for being a best friend, I would get one.

But Fern, well . . . I don't know if she would

get one. Best friends always save a seat for each other at lunch. And, now, well . . . Fern really isn't saving me a seat every day.

I thought about my rhyme real hard. I worked all morning. Teacher says sometimes words that rhyme look alike. So, here's some rhymes I wrote:

Please do not touch the couch.
Can you hear the bear?
Put the boot on the foot.

I was the only one who wrote *three* rhymes! But Teacher made his funny, scrunched-up-thinky face when I showed them to him. I know that face. And I know I don't like it.

"Well, Jo Jo, I'm sorry, but these don't work. They don't rhyme. You can work on this again after story time," Teacher said.

My face got very hot after he said that.

Fern whispered, "You look like a tomato, Jo Jo. Are you okay?"

The other kids in class looked at me. First

I felt my tummy get roll-y up and down. Then my lip quivered.

Then I thought about what Mama said this morning about me getting shots. I needed my best friend. My *other* one. My *home* best friend.

I thought about what Kokum said to me last night when she put me to bed. She told me a story about a very brave bear cub named

Little Makoons. And every morning Kokum also makes my hair into "bear hair." It is very cute.

She rubbed my tummy and whispered, "Oh, Little Makoons is rumbly in there tonight, my girl. I can hear it growling." Kokum kissed my cheek. "Maybe we should go get a snack to quiet Little Makoons?"

My tummy said "Yes!"

But I asked her, "Grandma, you have so many friends. How can I make *more* friends? It's kind of hard with some of the kids. You know, like when they are not very nice to me. Or if they don't want to sit with me at lunch every day."

Grandma answered, "Well, you don't have to try to be friends with everyone. But, my girl, you should try to be *friendly* with every-one."

I asked her, "You mean even Up-Chuck?"

She bopped my nose. "Oh, yes, Jo Jo. Being friendly can mean saying please and thank

you. Or it can mean you hold back from saying something not nice."

Yes, I thought. *I can do that. I will be very* friendly. *Friendly to make more friends! I will need more friends if Fern doesn't want to be my school best friend anymore.*

I cuddled with Mimi after Kokum left. Mimi licked my cheek. I like to sleep with her. But sometimes she snores.

4

The Cat Is Out of the Bag

When Teacher wasn't looking, I walked to the back of the room. That's where the coat cubbies are and all our backpacks are hung up. I quietly zipped mine open and reached in. "Oh, I'm so glad you're here," I whispered.

"Rmph," came from my backpack.

"Oh, *now* you're talking to me, Mimi? Okay, I forgive you for ignoring me this morning."

"Reooow." Her gray head stretched out of the backpack when I petted her.

"Shh, Mimi! Teacher doesn't know you're here. But I need you. I'm kind of sad. And kind of scared. You have to get shots or you can't go outside this summer."

"Puuuuurrrrrr."

"Mimi, remember when I had to get ouchie shots last year before kindergarten?"

"Puuuuurrrrrr."

"Okay, Mimi. Want to come sit with me?"

Mimi did not say no. I picked her up and tucked her into my shirt. We went back out to sit on the carpet for story time.

Teacher never even missed me. That was funny. But I wanted to see what he was talking about. I could hear him saying something about a tipi.

"Students, we have something very special in our classroom. As you know, our reservation museum will be hosting the Pembina Ojibwe Tribal tipi this summer," Teacher explained.

Teacher had his hand over a towel. It was covering something pointy on the table.

"And so, children, aren't we *so* lucky to have this? A miniature scale model for our room during this week!"

Teacher told us that every class in the school would get to have the tipi for a week. Then we could all have a special time learning about it.

He lifted the towel, and we all saw a tipi. It was about as big as my whole arm. It had little wooden poles and a tan deer hide stretched all around it. I'd like to have one like that at home! My dolls could fit their whole family in there! I would even let Spider-Man in it.

Then Teacher read to us from a picture book. I used to like this one. Fifteen reads ago. Teacher reads this book to us a lot. It's about a little girl scientist. But I couldn't listen the way I like to anyway because Mimi was clawing at me under my shirt.

Uh oh . . . Mimi crawled out of my shirt and she was on the run! I was sitting in the back row. The rest of the class didn't see a cat run across the carpet.

Except Fern. She saw it. "Oh no, Jo Jo!" she whispered.

The new girl, Susan, watched Mimi run to the tipi. But she didn't tell Teacher (like I know Brie, who is not a best friend, would). She gave me a side smile. Do you know what a side smile is? A side smile means you can keep a secret.

Whew. Okay, Mimi was safe. She'd just take a little cat nap in there. She likes little spaces. I could see her in the tipi from where

I was sitting. I thought I'd better scoot over to be closer.

Teacher was still reading the book. He seemed to like it so much. So we just kept watching and smiling.

I was keeping an eye on Mimi. She pawed around inside the tipi. I thought she was trying to get the fabric all squooshy and comfy for her nap.

"Oh no!" I whispered to Fern. You can tell secrets and worries to best friends. That is why I need a school best friend. Susan, the new girl, was keeping my Mimi secret. Would Fern, too?

I could see Mimi. I could see what she was doing in there.

Teacher noticed me talking during story time. He stopped reading.

"Jo Jo, why are you talking during story time?"

I said, "Oh, it's nothing, Teacher."

I made my eyes blink very fast. Fast blinking means you are very serious and full of truth. "No, sir. I'm good. I'm ready to listen," I answered.

Teacher set the book down on his lap. "No, Jo Jo, we'd really like to know what you told Fern."

I looked at Fern. I looked at Mimi. I looked at Teacher. He had that funny vein popping out on his forehead.

"Well, I . . . ," I said.

"Yeeesss, Jo Jo? What is it?" Teacher asked.

I said it as fast as I can. "Mimi went pee-pee in the tipi," I said with my shoulders hunched up.

"Oh, well, yes, Jo Jo. Yes. It's not the time for rhymes, really. But, okay, that works." I opened one eye to look at him. Teacher gave a little smile.

It was *okay* that my cat went pee-pee in the important tipi? I asked, "Are you sure, Teacher? It's okay?"

"Yes, Jo Jo, a little different, but it's all good," he answered.

"Soooo, it's okay?" I couldn't believe it! And Teacher never even looked at Mimi.

I rolled over and tried to grab my cat from inside the tipi.

I must have been talking to myself, because Teacher stopped reading. Again. "Hmm, what's that, Jo Jo? Something else to add?"

I stretched my arm inside the tipi to grab my cat.

"I can't reach her, Teacher," I said, all stretched out.

Teacher laughed with his mouth open. I could see his silver teeth in the back of his mouth. "Oh, Jo Jo, you certainly have learned wonderfully. Yes! Another good one."

"So," I began. "Is it okay?" I looked between Mimi and Teacher.

"Yes, Jo Jo. It's all *very* good. It's more than okay," Teacher said with a smile.

5

Jo Jo Knows

I learned a lot at school. Like, it's okay to bring your best cat friend to school. *And* it's okay if they have a bathroom "accident" in the classroom.

Luckily it was my week to be the student helper. This week I got to clean tables and water Teacher's plants. So I sneaked back to put Mimi in my backpack. I zipped it down so she could look out if she wanted to. Then I washed down tables. Quick-like, I wiped and cleaned up Mimi's pee-pee, then washed my hands. I checked, and Mimi was still in my backpack.

I was still scared about the shots. But I knew how to rhyme now!

And guess who got a *gold* star for 'creative rhyming'? *Me!* Me, thanks to Mimi. And the tipi and when she went . . . well, you know. I still like my other rhymes. Especially the "Please do not touch the couch" one. Maybe Mimi can help me teach Teacher about rhymes.

It was a Tuesday—my favorite day! The day we get to see Jim. He's so fun! There is always a new game to play with him.

"Okay, students, line up against the wall by the door," Teacher said right after math time.

Fern got to be the line leader. I was the last one in line—the caboose, Teacher calls it. Sometimes he calls it the "tail end" of the line.

Brie whispered to me, "Jo Jo is the *butt*

today. The butt of the line!"

I do not like Brie sometimes. So I stuck my tongue out at her. Except I didn't want to get in trouble, so I touched my tongue to my lip. That is being *friendly.*

Brie raised her hand and waved it around at Teacher. "Jo Jo stuck her tongue out at me!"

Real quick-like, I pretended I was licking my lips.

Teacher just looked at Brie, then me. He turned around and walked out the door to lead us down the hall. Rolling his eyes must mean he didn't believe her.

We walked by all the big kid rooms. Like third grade. The third-grade teacher always keeps the door shut so we can't see in. Third grade must be very scary if they don't want the rest of us to see what's going on in there.

Finally, we got to Jim's door. Fern led us in. We high-fived Jim when we walked past him. I was the last one (because I'm the caboose today) and said, "Hi, Jim!"

Jim looked down at me and laughed. He bent down next to me. "Boozhoo, Jo Jo! Hey, why do you always call me Jim?"

I looked up at him. Doesn't he know his own name?

"Well, because that's what Teacher calls you. Every Tuesday he says, 'Okay, class, let's line up and go to Jim.' And then we walk down to see you, Jim."

Jim patted my head and laughed. "Jo Jo, you do know that this is *gym* class. Yes, you all walk down to *gym* class—G-Y-M. In the gym. And my name is Antoine Morin. Do you hear the other kids call me Mr. Morin?"

I felt my face getting all tomato red again. I guess I never noticed that.

I walked by him into the *gym*. He laughed real nice-like again and said so only I could hear, "But, Jo Jo, you can still call me Jim."

Jim is my favorite teacher.

Jo Jo's Class Yearbook

Later that afternoon, Teacher made a *very* big announcement.

"Students, the principal, Ms. Whirl Wind Horse, is letting *our* grade help design the school's yearbook. Isn't that exciting, children?"

Brie, said, "Oh, how fun!" Last week I asked Brie what her name means. She told me, "I am named after a very fancy cheese, Jo Jo." I do not know if I like cheese anymore.

Ferris started clapping. Ferris is my bus friend. Sometimes I ask him for a favor—to switch seats so I can sit by the window. He always says yes.

Well, what's the big deal? Who cares about a book on grass and dirt? So I asked, "Teacher, what's a yard book?"

All at once, the class turned to me with big eyes. Then one person in the back started to laugh. Then almost everyone, even Teacher, laughed real loud. At me.

I couldn't see Fern because she was in front of me. But I know for sure I didn't see Lilly laugh. I've always liked that Lilly. She is very friendly to me.

"Oh, Jo Jo, it's not a yard book, it's a *year*-book. You know, where all the student pictures in the school are included. A yearbook also has things that happened over the entire school year," Teacher said.

"Jo Jo, it's like a memory book of the school. You didn't know that?" Chuck giggled.

No, Up-Chuck, I did not. But that is not what I said out loud. Sometimes it's good to keep practicing being friendly. Like now. Like when I did not pull his braid on the bus this morning because I really tried my best to be *friendly*. It is very hard sometimes.

Teacher explained, "And so, class, Ms. Whirl Wind Horse has asked that any student may submit artwork for the yearbook. They are due Friday."

"Just think, we could have our art in a book!" Brie squealed.

"Yes, Brie," Teacher replied. "Remember, a yearbook's artwork is a way to use pictures showing the students' school-year experiences and memories."

And that is when I decided I would like to have my art in a book, too.

I worked all week on my YEARbook pictures. And I did not include any yard pictures at all. Teacher said we need to explain the students in art. So that is what I did. I drew how I will remember my class from this school year.

I included all the students in my class. This is how I was being friendly to *all* of them. Even Brie. They will all have special artwork all about them.

I kept my fingers crossed all day so my art would be picked. But it was very hard to brush my teeth with my fingers crossed that night. I *knew* the principal would pick my art for the yearbook. My art is very special!

Even Mimi thought so when I showed it to her at home. Well, she never said she *didn't* like it.

Shots Ahoy

After school I decided to spy on Mama and Grandma because they've been whispering a lot lately. Mimi is a very smart kitty. She knows the *v* word. When she hears the word *vet*, she runs and hides. She does not like the vet.

I could hear them saying "shots soon." And "need to trick her." I needed to tell Mimi to be brave when she gets her shots.

So I crawled under the round dining room table that has a long tablecloth on it.

45

"She won't like it," Mama whispered.

"Well," Kokum replied, "who does like shots? But today's the day."

Mama sighed. "I guess I'll go get her into the car."

I held my breath under the table for about twenty-five minutes. Or at least it felt that long. Maybe it was only a minute? But I had my mind made up. If Mimi was getting shots, I needed to give her a very big hug. And to tell her to hold her breath so she does not lose all her air.

I heard Mama and Kokum get up and walk around the house. Then I heard the garage door open. Then close after a car went out. So I peeked out from under the table. I wondered, *where is Mimi?* I heard the car back out of the driveway. I ran to the front door.

Boom! I ran right into Kokum.

"Oh, Jo Jo, where are you running to so fast?" Kokum asked.

"Er, well . . ." I glanced out the window to see Mama driving away slowly.

"Kokum, is Mimi in the car?" I asked.

"Well, yes, for her shots, my girl," Grandma answered.

I said, "But I didn't get to give her a hug to be brave. That is what best friends do."

"No, Jo Jo, Mimi is already very brave. I'm more nervous for the vet!" she said with a laugh.

Sometimes I wonder about Kokum's way of

thinking and remembering things. It is very funny. Why would she worry about the vet? Mimi is the one who got shots!

Meow-ouch! I sent her all my heart kisses to protect her.

The next morning, I remembered that Teacher said we had to turn in our drawings for the *yearbook*. I grabbed my stack of drawings from the kitchen table and walked out the front door.

"Bye, Mimi!" I said, very full of love to her.

Mimi did not answer me. I know she did not like getting her shots. But the vet must have been very good because Mimi did not lose all her air either. I told Ferris later, "Shots are not very fun, but they are good for us all. Ferris, I thought you were very smart about air and balloons. But you are not."

Shots are not fun. At all. But maybe they are not that scary because they are over very fast, and they help us to be healthy. Maybe they should call shots "vitamins." Or maybe Mimi is very brave.

Ferris is a good bus friend, and I was being *friendly* by telling him the truth. That he is not as smart as he thought.

Fern was waiting for me at school by the front door. I hoped she would sit by me at lunch. I wondered if she would act like my best school friend today.

"Boozhoo, Jo Jo!" Fern said. She said it with a smile, so I think today she will be a school best friend. "Did you bring your art?"

"Boozhoo, Fern!" I answered. "Yes, I have a whole big stack of my art. Look!"

Fern's eyes got very big. "Wow, Jo Jo. I know Ms. Whirl Wind Horse will pick yours." Remember, fast blinking means you are very serious and full of truth.

"Oh, Fern, do you think?" I asked.

We walked into our classroom together.

Up-Chuck was ahead of us talking to Teacher in the doorway.

"Boozhoo, Fern. Boozhoo, Jo Jo," Teacher said.

Up-Chuck was smiling big at Fern. Were they school best friends now? My heart felt very droopy thinking about that.

I sort of dropped one of my art papers in front of Teacher. I wanted Up-Chuck to get away from *my* school best friend, Fern.

"Oh," I said real loud-like, lip-pointing to the floor. "Can you pick that up, Chuck?"

Teacher looked at me with squinty eyes. I could see his forehead vein popping out again. Up-Chuck just laughed and handed me my paper.

Teacher looked at me, so I smiled big. Kokum told me a big smile is what friends give to each other. I even tucked my lips under so he could see my gums. A gum smile means I am not being mean to Up-Chuck by calling him Up-Chuck.

But why is Teacher's forehead vein getting bigger and bulgier?

So quickly I added, "Can you pick that up, Chuck . . . *please*?" Using *please* is being *friendly*.

Jo Jo's Friends

Today the principal, Ms. Whirl Wind Horse, decided on the art for the yearbook.

Teacher walked us down to the big G-Y-M for the announcement.

I am very good at A-R-T. So I can't wait to hear my name get called as the winner.

Fern saved me a spot on the floor. We sat together with the other first graders. I sat down and reached for Fern's hand. Best friends like to hold hands.

But on the other side of Fern I saw Susan.

And Susan was holding Fern's other hand. My eyes felt like little pokey things were jabbing me. I tried to stick my tongue out to catch a big fat tear. But more fat tears kept falling.

"Jo Jo," Fern whispered in my ear. "Are you okay?"

I am not okay. My school best friend has so many *other* school best friends. I tried to give her a very big gum smile. But it did not look pretty because my tears kept making my lips slip back over my teeth.

"Shh, girls!" Teacher said to us. "Ms. Whirl

Wind Horse is announcing the yearbook art winner."

The principal cleared her throat. "Thank you very much to all the students who submitted their art for the yearbook."

Fern squeezed my hand. I squeezed hers back. I knew Susan did not get a Fern squeeze. At least, I didn't think so.

"And so, children," the principal continued, "let's all clap loudly for the winner . . . Waaban Gladue. Waaban is in the fourth grade and has drawn a beautiful butterfly. It will be on the yearbook cover."

The principal showed us all the butterfly picture.

Everyone clapped. Everyone except me. I knew it was important to be happy for others. So finally I slipped my hand from Fern's and clapped. But I did not put *all* my love into my clap.

Waaban drew a very good butterfly. She was in the fourth grade. I knew third grade was scary, but fourth grade must be okay. But my big fat tears came even faster now.

I tucked my chin very close to my neck to make myself smaller. I could see something waving next to my face.

"Here, Jo Jo, take this," someone said in my ear.

I looked up and tried to wipe my eyes so I could see.

Brie waved a tissue by my face. "You can wipe your eyes, Jo Jo." Brie's head was tilted and her eyes were big. She patted my arm and said, "Jo Jo, I think your art was prettier than the butterfly."

Wow! Brie was being very *friendly* to *me*. I nodded to her and took the tissue.

But just in case it had boogers on it, I tucked it into my pocket. I wiped my eyes on my shirt. Except I did it all sneaky-like to not hurt Brie's feelings.

I am getting very good at being *friendly*. Even to Brie.

* * *

Later that day at lunch I walked to Fern's and my usual table. But she wasn't there. I could see her sitting next to Up-Chuck. And Brie. And Susan. And Lilly (I've always liked that Lilly).

I could feel my prickly-eye pokey thing starting again. So I started to turn to sit with my back to them. All by myself.

Then, right then, I saw Up-Chuck lip-point to me. Then he lip-pointed to the empty seat next to all of them. At *their* lunch table.

Suddenly my prickly, pokey eyes stopped. I walked over to their table.

"Jo Jo," Fern said, "I'm so happy you want to sit with us. I missed you."

I answered, right in Fern's ear, "But I thought you didn't want to be best friends anymore."

I must have said it too loud because everyone started saying things.

"Jo Jo, we always saved a seat here for you!" Up-Chuck said.

Susan added, "Yeah, Jo Jo, you always make us laugh."

Then, Brie said, "Jo Jo, I thought you didn't like me, or us."

My cheeks stretched so long! I was very happy and tried to give them all my biggest gum smile.

I sat down across from Fern. And without us even talking, she took my sandwich (tuna fish—P.U.!). Fern gave me her peanut butter and jelly sandwich.

Only best friends trade stinky tuna fish.

And my other new friendly friends plugged their noses very politely as Fern ate it.

The next week Teacher called me over to his desk at quiet reading time.

"Jo Jo," he began. Teacher was not being very quiet during quiet reading time.

"Jo Jo," Teacher continued, "I took one of your yearbook art pictures. I sent it to my friend at our reservation museum."

I looked at Teacher's forehead. His vein always lets me know how he's really feeling. No sticky-outie vein. This must be good news.

"Jo Jo, the museum director liked one of your pieces of art very much. She is going to use it for the poster for the Pembina Tribal tipi this summer!"

"Gosh," I said. "I *am* an artist!"

And that is why my art is on the poster all over the reservation. It is very funny art, though. I wonder if they saw *everything* in my picture.

When I grabbed all my yearbook art last week from my kitchen table, one must have gotten stuck in that pile. One that was not a yearbook art picture.

But, now all of my best friends and new friendly friends can see my art.

༻✿ JO JO'S GLOSSARY ✿༺

A glossary is a very fancy word for a small dictionary. It is where you can learn new words and how to say them. For the Ojibwe words I used the Ojibwe People's Dictionary from the University of Minnesota.

Here are some Ojibwe and Michif words from this story:

boozhoo (BOO-zhoo): hello, greetings.

kokum (KUH-kum): Michif word for grandma

moushoom (MUH-shoom): Michif word for grandpa

makoons (ma-KOONS): little bear cub

nindizhinikaaz (nin-DEZH-in-i-kauz): my name is . . .

Ojibwe (oh-JIB-way): the name of my Native American Nation

❧ AUTHOR'S NOTE ❧

The Ojibwe people belong to many Bands (or groups) and Nations. I am part of the Pembina Band of Ojibwe. My reservation is the Turtle Mountain Reservation in North Dakota. It is the current land for the Turtle Mountain Band of Ojibwe.

The Ojibwe Nations are within the borders of the United States and Canada. Some of our Ojibwe reservations are within the borders of North Dakota, Wisconsin, Minnesota, and Michigan. Just like Jo Jo said, we speak Ojibwe, but also many other dialects, or versions, of it. My Turtle Mountain reservation uses Ojibwe and Michif.

Dear Reader,

Do you love to laugh? I do, and I adore big personalities like Jo Jo Makoons Azure!

What fun to meet a good-hearted, funny character like her in the pages of a book!

I especially love how her sense of humor springs from her life at home, in school, and in her tribal community. Jo Jo is quite the character, isn't she? Just by being herself, she offers us a peek into her high-spirited day-to-day hijinks and the way her busy brain works. Like many of us, she tries her best to figure things out, even when the world feels confusing and strange.

And here's some terrific news—this is only the first book about her adventures!

Have you read other stories about young Ojibwe heroes like Jo Jo? How about young heroes from other Native or First Nations? I hope this book inspires you to read more.

Jo Jo Makoons: The Used-to-be Best Friend is written by the brilliant and hilarious Dawn Quigley, illustrated by the amazing and imaginative Tara Audibert, and published by Heartdrum, a Native-focused imprint of HarperCollins Children's Books. An imprint is like a little umbrella under the bigger umbrella of a publishing company. Under our little umbrella, we publish stories by Native writers and artists about Native heroes who are kids like you.

I've met some of my best friends in books, and I hope you'll think of yourself as Jo Jo's friend, too. Be sure to look for more books in the series!

Thank you for reading,
Cynthia Leitich Smith

DAWN QUIGLEY is a citizen of the Turtle Mountain Band of Ojibwe, North Dakota. Her debut YA novel, *Apple in the Middle*, was awarded an American Indian Youth Literature Honor. She is a PhD education university faculty member and a former K–12 reading and English teacher, as well as Indian Education program codirector. You can find her online at www.dawnquigley.com.

TARA AUDIBERT is a multidisciplinary artist, filmmaker, cartoonist, animator, and podcaster. She owns and runs Moxy Fox Studio, where she creates her award-winning works, including the animated short film *The Importance of Dreaming*, comics *This Place: 150 Years Retold* and *Lost Innocence*, and "Nitap: Legends of the First Nations," an animated storytelling app. She is of Wolastoqey/French heritage and resides in Sunny Corner, New Brunswick, Canada. You can find her online at www.moxyfox.ca.

CYNTHIA LEITICH SMITH is the bestselling, acclaimed author of books for all ages, including *Rain Is Not My Indian Name*, *Indian Shoes*, *Jingle Dancer*, and *Hearts Unbroken*, which won the American Indian Library Association's Youth Literature Award; she is also the anthologist of *Ancestor Approved: Intertribal Stories for Kids*. Most recently, she was named the 2021 NSK Neustadt Laureate. Cynthia is the author-curator of Heartdrum, a Native-focused imprint at HarperCollins Children's Books, and serves as the Katherine Paterson Inaugural Endowed Chair on the faculty of the MFA program in Writing for Children and Young Adults at Vermont College of Fine Arts. She is a citizen of the Muscogee (Creek) Nation and lives in Austin, Texas. You can visit Cynthia online at www.cynthialeitichsmith.com.

In 2014, **WE NEED DIVERSE BOOKS** (WNDB) began as a simple hashtag on Twitter. The social media campaign soon grew into a 501(c)(3) nonprofit with a team that spans the globe. WNDB is supported by a network of writers, illustrators, agents, editors, teachers, librarians, and book lovers, all united under the same goal—to create a world where every child can see themselves in the pages of a book. You can learn more about WNDB programs at www.diversebooks.org.